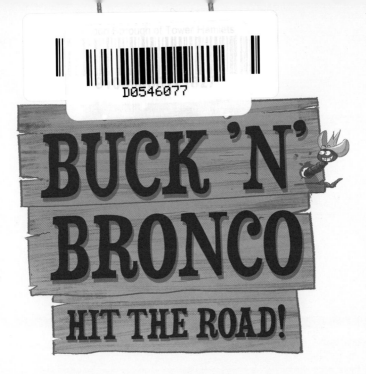

BUCK 'N' BRONCO

HIT THE ROAD!

GUY BASS

Illustrated by
STEVE MAY

Barrington Stoke

To Abraham and Leonard

First published in 2021 in Great Britain by
Barrington Stoke Ltd
18 Walker Street, Edinburgh, EH3 7LP

www.barringtonstoke.co.uk

Text © 2021 Guy Bass
Illustrations © 2021 Steve May

A CIP catalogue record for this book is available
from the British Library upon request

ISBN: 978-1-78112-972-2

Printed by Hussar Books, Poland

CONTENTS

WELCOME TO HAPPY

Welcome to Happy Ranch theme park, where fun comes first!

Ride our rockin' rides all day with our "All Rides, All Day" ride pass!

ROCKIN ROLLER

FUN! FUN!

RANCH!

Topsy-turvy roller coasters! Curvy swervy! Don't be nervy!

What a happy day! What a happy stay! What a happy place to come and play!

HOT DOGS

BRONCO

Here at Happy Ranch, it's our job to make your day as happy as can be, with our marvellous mascots, Buck 'n' Bronco! It's their singing, dancing mascot mission to Bring the Happy™ to your day!

BUCK: I'm Buck!

BRONCO: And I'm Bronco!

BUCK: Take a chance on the ranch! Do the Buck 'n' Bronco dance!

BRONCO: Let us *Bring the Happy* to your day, because if you ain't happy …

BUCK: … We're not happy!

THAT WAS THEN ...

... THIS IS NOW.

Chapter 1
Goodbye, Happy Ranch

*"We're mascots – and mascots need
a theme park!"*

The rusty old Happy Ranch sign hung over the entrance to the park, creaking slowly in the summer breeze. Another sign had been stuck over it.

PARK CLOSED DOWN

"Closed down?" Buck howled. His eyes popped out of his head on stalks. "What in the name

of hot dogs and candy floss is going on? They can't shut Happy Ranch!"

"Shucks, Buck, we're outta luck," Bronco sighed. "Maybe we should have seen this comin' – we ain't had no one visitin' the park these past weeks ..."

"Why, we've had *plenty* of visitors," Buck replied. He wracked his brain. "There was, uh ... and there was ... and, uh ..."

"There was that old lady who stopped to ask for directions to the nearest gas station," Bronco said helpfully.

"It's the quiet season, is all!" Buck snapped. "We never get as many human folk this month."

"I dunno, Buck, this month seems to have lasted all year," Bronco said with another sigh. "We ain't had a payin' customer in forever."

"That's no reason to close the park!" Buck said. "Ugh, this *stinks*."

"Sorry, Buck," Bronco muttered as he tried to sniff his own bottom.

"I'm not talking about your pony pong, Bronco," Buck replied. "We both know that you can't break wind unless I pull your finger." Buck pointed at the sign. "I'm talking about this! 'Park Closed Down' ... Can you think of three unkinder words in all the English language?"

Bronco rubbed his chin and said, "Demolition in Progress?"

"What are you talking about?" said Buck, looking up at his friend.

Bronco pointed to another sign right next to them, on a wooden post dug into the ground. It read:

DEMOLITION IN PROGRESS!

"What's that doing there?" Buck asked. "Crank my antlers! They can't demolish the—"

"Buck, duck!" Bronco cried.

A shadow fell over them. A moment later, a huge iron wrecking ball flew over their heads and crashed into the main gates of the theme park.

Buck 'n' Bronco leapt away as a small army of bulldozers rumbled inside the park. They began smashing and flattening ride after ride, stall after stall. Soon there was nothing left of Happy Ranch but rubble and dust.

"I love the smell of bulldozing in the morning!" a man declared as he strode out of the dust towards Buck 'n' Bronco. He took off his yellow hard hat and breathed in deeply. "Smells like ... *progress*."

"What have you *done*?" Buck howled. "I don't know if you noticed, but I'm a cartoonish

stag and Bronco here is more or less a pony! We're *mascots* – and mascots need a theme park!"

"Calm down, *deer*," the man replied. He pulled the DEMOLITION IN PROGRESS sign out of the ground. "This old park was about to fall down all by itself anyway."

"That ain't so!" Bronco protested. "Happy Ranch had a rustic charm. Sure, it could have done with a lick of paint ... a few repairs ... some pest control, maybe ..."

"The point is, you demolished our *home*," Buck snarled at the man. "What are we supposed to do now?"

"I don't know about the pony, but it's hunting season for deer," the man replied with a grin.

"*Hunting season?*" Buck gasped. "I'm not some wild animal destined for the dinner table – I walk on two legs! I have opposable thumbs! I wear a waistcoat, for pity's sake! WE ARE MASCOTS!"

"You got a problem?" the man said. "Take it up with the management." With that, he shoved another sign into the earth. It read:

OPENING SOON:

ALISON WUNDERLAND'S
ISLANDS OF TOMORROW
THE THEME PARK OF THE FUTURE, TODAY!

Chapter 2
Branding

*"Why don't we take that bus of
yours out on the road?"*

Buck 'n' Bronco stared at the Islands of
Tomorrow sign and their jaws both dropped to
the ground with a loud THUD! The sign showed
a picture of a theme park. It was like nothing
they had ever seen before.

There were bright silver roller coasters
that seemed to stretch into the clouds ...
Whirling, twirling water slides, snaking

and criss-crossing this way and that ...
Helter-skelters that shimmered in the
sunshine ... And countless flying drones
delivering food and drink to happy children.

It looked like someone had dreamed of the
perfect theme park and drawn it right there on
that sign.

Bronco picked up his jaw from the floor.

"Shucks, Buck, that there's one tip-top
lookin' park," he said.

"Oh, *sure* it's flashy, but where's the fun?"
Buck huffed. "How's anyone supposed to Bring
the Happy in a park so prim 'n' polished?
Crank my antlers, if I ever meet that Alison
Blunderland I'm going to give her a piece of
my mind ..."

"Maybe we could apply to be mascots for
the Islands of Tomorrow?" Bronco suggested.

"Bite your tongue, Bronco Trotter," Buck said. "A place like that doesn't deserve mascots like us. Why, that Theme Park of the Future is the reason we don't *have* a future! No home, no job, no nothing!"

"We've still got the Bronco Bus," said Bronco. He turned towards the Happy Ranch car park and pointed at a brightly coloured bus complete with a mane and pony's tail. "It ain't no good for drivin' round the park singin' our Happy Ranch song no more, what with the park not bein' there. But we could live in it instead!"

"*Live* in it?" Buck scoffed. "I'm Buck Stops, one half of the greatest mascot duo since Hot Dog 'n' Mustard! I can't live in a motor vehicle! I've got a better idea – why don't we take that bus of yours out on the road?"

"You mean … out there, in the world beyond Happy Ranch?" said Bronco nervously.

"Why not?" replied Buck. "We may never have left the ranch, but I'll bet twenty Buck's Bucks that our *legend* has spread far and wide. Why, I'll bet every kid in the world goes to bed saying, 'Shucks, Momma, I sure wish Buck 'n' Bronco weren't stuck inside Happy Ranch so I could meet 'em!' I'll bet folk out there will be desperate to make us mascots of all sorts! Bigger theme parks … better theme parks!"

"But … there ain't no better theme park than Happy Ranch," said Bronco with a sniff.

"Don't you get it?" said Buck. "This is our chance to *branch out of the ranch*. You see the mark on your rump there?"

Buck glanced down at the two large letters on his bottom:

B&B

"B&B ... For Buck 'n' Bronco," said Bronco proudly.

"Exactly!" said Buck, showing off an identical "B&B" on his own backside. "You know what that is, old buddy? *Branding*. And branding is everything! You want to stumble around in the dark all your life?"

"I confess I ain't a fan of the dark, Buck," Bronco said.

"Which is why we need to be in the spotlight every minute of the day!" said Buck. "The whole *point* of a mascot is that everybody knows who you are … and this is our chance! We can take the Buck 'n' Bronco brand to a whole new set of human folk!"

"So, you're sayin' we could Bring the Happy to even more folk than before?" asked Bronco with a giddy whinny.

"I'm saying we could be famous again," Buck said. "We could be *mascots* again. There's no time to lose, pony – Buck 'n' Bronco are hitting the road!"

Chapter 3
On the Road

*"The world beyond Happy Ranch is
like one big, round theme park."*

The Bronco Bus rode slowly down the highway,
its engine noise a chugging chuckle. "Dip my
antlers in candy floss!" Buck gasped. "I can
hardly believe what I'm seeing!"

The theme park had been their home for as
long as they could remember, and the outside
world seemed to go on *forever*.

Green fields stretched out all around. Behind them loomed a wide and towering mountain range on the horizon, and ahead a distant city gleamed with countless silver skyscrapers.

"I ... I ain't sure this is such a good idea, Buck," Bronco said. He kept his eyes on the road as his tail swished nervously behind him. "This place is bigger than a hundred Happy Ranches ... Where's the Entrance and Exit?"

"There *are* no entrances and exits, Bronco," explained Buck. "The world beyond Happy Ranch is like one big, round theme park. Why, it's bound to be filled to bursting with opportunities for two famous mascots like you and me ... I don't know why we didn't think of leaving sooner!"

"Happy Ranch always seemed plenty big enough to me," said Bronco. "Where do we even start to Bring the Happy in a place with all this bigness?"

"Bronco Trotter, now is not the time to be a nervous nag," said Buck. "Trust me, the human folk are going to be climbing over themselves to make us mascots. All we need to do is find us some ..."

"That could be a problem," said Bronco, checking the fuel indicator on the Bronco Bus's dashboard. "The tank is nearly empty – how are we goin' to fill up with laughin' gas when we ain't got a penny to our name?"

"Don't panic, pony," Buck replied. "Your old buddy Buck has thought of everything ..." Buck took out a handful of bank notes from his waistcoat. Each one had a picture of his grinning face on one side and one of Bronco on the other.

"Buck's Bucks?" gasped Bronco. "I ain't never seen so much! Where'd you get all that money?"

"Back at the ranch, of course," replied Buck. "I swiped it from the gift shop before they shut us down. They may have taken our home, Bronco, but with this we can start again!"

"I dunno, Buck," Bronco said. "Are you sure we can even *spend* Buck's Bucks out here?"

"I love you, Bronco, but you are one pessimistic pony," said Buck as he pocketed the Buck's Bucks. "This could be the best thing that ever happened to ... Wait! Hit the brakes!"

Bronco stamped on the Bronco-brakes and the Bronco Bus skidded to a tuneful stop.

"What's up, Buck?" asked Bronco.

"*Look*," Buck said. He pointed to a sign on the side of the road that read:

WUNDERVILLE
TOWN OF THE FUTURE
NEXT EXIT

"Shucks, Buck, ain't that a stroke of luck?" Bronco said. "We can fill up the tank there."

"We're going to do a whole lot more than that, pal o' mine," Buck said. "A town means human folk, and human folk is all we need to get us back in the mascot business!"

"*Wunderville*," repeated Bronco. "I wonder if it's got anythin' to do with Alison Wunderland ...?"

"Don't even say that name!" Buck said. "Alison *Blunderland* and her puffed-up park are not worth wasting one breath on. Trust me, this town's going to be the first stop on our comeback tour! It's the start of a glorious new chapter for Buck Stops and Bronco Trotter! There's no time to lose – thataway, Bronco, thataway!"

Chapter 4
Welcome to Wunderville

"Robots, Buck – actual robots!"

It was late afternoon when the Bronco Bus
rolled into Wunderville. If Buck 'n' Bronco had
been asked to imagine the most charming town
in the history of charming towns, they would
have imagined Wunderville.

The streets were bright and clean, and the
colourful houses had wide, neat front lawns.
The air smelled sweet – but not the candy
floss and ketchup sweetness that had filled

their nostrils at Happy Ranch. This smell was wholesome and healthy, like flowers and fresh-cut grass.

"Shucks, Buck, it's all so ... *shiny*," said Bronco, looking out of the side window. His eyes bulged as he saw a small robotic truck roll past them along the road, sucking up litter as it went. A moment later, they spotted another robot on the lawn of a nearby house, mowing the grass ... then another rolling up to a door to drop off bags full of shopping. "Robots, Buck – actual robots!" Bronco gasped. "You reckon this is what the whole world is like?"

"I'll tell you what I reckon, Bronco, old chum," Buck replied excitedly. "This here Wunderville is some sort of super-modern future town that's not even been invented yet!"

"Future ...?" said Bronco. "Say, Buck, do you think this here *town of the future* has anything to do with that there Theme Park of the—"

"Hold that thought, pony – I smell human folk," said Buck as his nostrils grew to the size of dinner plates.

They rounded a corner into a wide town square lined with flowerbeds being pruned by floating robot drones. The square was filled with townsfolk making their way here and there while greeting each other with a smile and a wave and a "How do you do?"

"Thataway, old buddy," Buck said. "It's been a long time since I heard the grateful laughter and adoring cheers of human folk."

Bronco steered the bus straight into the square, running over a flowerbed in the process. "I'll bet twenty Buck's Bucks that the humans are all asking themselves the same question," Buck continued. "Is that *really* Buck 'n' Bronco? Can it be that the one and only Happy Ranch mascots have come to our little old town?"

"I dunno, Buck," said Bronco. "Shucks, I ain't even sure they've noticed we're here."

"Then it's high time we introduced ourselves ..." said Buck with a grin.

The Bronco Bus finally chuckled and spluttered to a halt in the middle of the square and Buck leapt out of it, heading towards a gathering of townsfolk.

"Buck, wait! I can't park here!" Bronco cried. He tried to restart the Bronco Bus as Buck made a beeline for the nearest family. It was a mum and dad, who were admiring the flowers, and a little girl, who was gazing at her bright blue helium balloon.

"A happy howdy to you!" cried Buck, cartwheeling in front of the family.

The girl screamed with surprise.

"Say, now!" the dad yelled. "What's the big idea, sneaking up on us like that?"

"Sneaking?" Buck said. "Who's sneaking? It's me, Buck!"

The family stared at Buck with the same look of confusion. The mum gave a small shrug.

"You know, Buck Stops, from Happy Ranch!" Buck continued. "Shoot, get over here, Bronco! These poor folks need the full picture ..."

Bronco left the Bronco Bus and cantered across the square, skidding to a halt beside his friend.

"Sorry, Buck," Bronco panted. "The Bronco Bus is well and truly—"

"Never mind that!" said Buck, and pointed up at Bronco with a grin. "Human folk of Wunderville, your eyes don't lie – it's us! The world's greatest mascots, Buck 'n' Bronco!"

There was a long pause. At last the girl with the balloon spoke.

It was then that Buck 'n' Bronco heard words they had never heard before – words they had not imagined they would *ever* hear.

"Who are Buck 'n' Bronco?" the girl said.

Chapter 5

Who Are Buck 'n' Bronco?

*"This town's more topsy-turvy than
the Rockin' Roller Coaster!"*

"WHO ARE BUCK 'N' BRONCO?" Buck howled.
Steam shot out of his ears, accompanied by a
loud whistling sound. The girl chuckled. "What
do you mean, 'Who are Buck 'n' Bronco'?" Buck
continued.

"You – you ain't never heard of us?" Bronco
asked with a confused whinny.

The mum and dad both shrugged.

"Doesn't ring a bell," the dad confessed. "Are you two fellas new in town?"

"Well, yes – but that's hardly the point," Buck huffed. "You've been to Happy Ranch theme park, right? Why, it can't be an hour's drive from here!"

"I'm sorry," replied the mum. "I've never even heard of this 'Happy Place'."

"Ranch! Happy Ranch!" Buck said. "Dip me in batter and call me a corn dog, you folks need your memories jogging. There's only one thing for it, pony – it's time for the Buck 'n' Bronco Dance."

Buck gave his friend a thumbs up as more townsfolk gathered around. In an instant, Bronco began tapping his feet on the spot and waving his arms back and forth. After a moment, Buck joined in and the pair sang at the top of their lungs:

> Do the Buck 'n' Bronco dance!
> Fun, fun, fun at the Happy Ranch!
> Laugh and play and sing along
> We Bring the Happy all day long!

Buck 'n' Bronco's legs whirled and spun like helicopter blades as they danced. By now, a crowd of locals were watching them. Buck 'n' Bronco grinned at each other.

"Just like the old days!" cried Bronco. "Second verse?"

"Second verse, old buddy!" replied Buck – and on they sang:

> Do the Buck 'n' Bronco dance!
> Stop the fun? We simply can't!
> Yippee yay and whoop dee doo!
> Bringin' Happy is what we do!

"Time for the big Buck 'n' Bronco finish!" Buck cried.

> *Do the Buck 'n' Bronco dance!*
> *Laugh until you wet your pants!*
> *For a second longer, linger!*
> *Time to pull on Bronco's finger!*

Bronco held out his index finger, Buck took hold of it – and pulled.

PAAAAARRRRRP!

The force of Bronco's gigantic fart launched him high into the air! He blasted skywards like a rocket, higher and higher, until he seemed to disappear into the glare of the sun ... Then, suddenly, he plummeted back to earth with a

FWEEEEEEEEEEEEEEE ...

DOIMP!

PARRP!

"See? It's ... really ... us!" Buck panted as Bronco fell flat on his back, exhausted.

By now the girl was giggling so much she almost let go of her balloon. Buck didn't even notice – he was staring at the girl's parents, who looked even more confused than before.

"... Like I said, none of this is ringing a bell," said the dad.

Buck peered past the family to the crowd. Everyone was muttering to each other, not sure what to make of these strange visitors.

"Don't *any* of y'all know who we are?" asked Bronco, getting to his feet. The crowd shrugged, one after another – a Mexican wave of shrugging, until no shoulder was left un-shrugged.

Buck turned to Bronco, covered his mouth with his hand and whispered, "These folks must have been living under a rock. I've got a feeling

Wunderville isn't as up to date and modern as you thought, pal. Maybe we should try the next town ..."

"But, Buck, the bus is bust," replied Bronco. "We ain't going nowhere without a full tank of laughin' gas."

"Well, I'm not staying here any longer than we have to," hissed Buck. He took a wad of cash out of his waistcoat and waved it at the crowd. "A hundred Buck's Bucks to whoever can get us ten gallons of laughing gas!"

"What are 'Buck's Bucks'?" the mum asked. "Is that like crypto currency?"

"Crisp-oh what now?" Buck replied. "Ma'am, I haven't the first clue what you're talking about ..."

"I ... I think she might be sayin' Buck's Bucks ain't real money, Buck," said Bronco.

"What?" cried Buck. "This town's more topsy-turvy than the Rockin' Roller Coaster! Next you'll be telling me we're not famous *anywhere* in this whole crazy—"

"Buck 'n' Bronco?" said a voice behind them.

"At *last*, somebody knows us," Buck whispered. He and Bronco spun on their heels, with wide toothy grins on their faces. "A happy howdy to you!" Buck cried. "I'm Buck and this here is my ... good ... pal ..."

Buck trailed off as he found himself staring into the face of a *robot*. The metallic figure towered over Buck on long legs below a round, bucket-like body. Its chest displayed a gold badge with the words "WUNDERCOP #5".

Buck looked up at the robot's face, which was just a curve of silver metal. It was so well polished that Bronco could see a crooked reflection of his own worried face in it.

"You are Bronco P. Trotter, are you not?" said the robot.

"Yes! Buck 'n' Bronco, that's us!" Buck laughed, throwing his arm around Bronco. "It's good to finally meet someone who knows their antler from their elbow! I don't want to bad mouth the locals, but they don't seem to have the first clue who we—"

"That vehicle is registered in your name, Mr Trotter," the robot interrupted Buck, pointing a thin metal arm at the Bronco Bus. "Vehicles are not permitted in Tomorrow Square. You need to move it."

Buck slapped his palm against his forehead and ground his teeth together so hard that sparks shot out across the square.

"Is this about *parking?*" Buck groaned.

"We ran out of laughin' gas, officer," Bronco explained as his knees started to knock together with nerves. "The bus ain't parked so much as *stuck* there."

"Then you have a problem," said the robot.

"Weren't you listening?" snapped Buck.
He jabbed the robot with his finger. "We're not going anywhere!"

"And now you have another problem," said the robot. "You're under arrest."

Chapter 6
Alison Wunderland

*"I feel like I've waited my whole life
to see you again."*

"That went south real fast," Bronco sighed as the door to their jail cell slammed shut.

It was twenty minutes since Buck 'n' Bronco had been arrested. Buck hadn't even had time to cry, "You can't do this to us – we're mascots, beloved by children and adults alike!" before they'd found themselves behind bars in Wunderville police headquarters.

"We've got a problem, Buck," said Bronco. His tail swished as he glanced nervously around the cell.

"You *think?*" screeched Buck. "In the last few hours, we lost our jobs, our home was demolished, our bus ran out of gas and we found out our money isn't even money. Now we're locked away like a couple of criminals, because that's *exactly what we are*! What problem, Bronco? I don't see a problem!"

"Well, I've been thinkin'," replied Bronco. "How on earth are we goin' to Bring the Happy if we're stuck in here?"

"*Bring the Happy?*" Buck boomed. "Look at us, we're jailbirds! Who cares about Bringing the dang Happy?"

"Shucks, Buck, I guess *I* do," replied Bronco. "I ain't Brought the Happy in forever. Givin' that girl with the balloon a chuckle was the best thing that's happened to me in too long."

"Making one kid laugh?" Buck huffed. "That's hardly a busy day at the office. We have to face facts – I'm a buck out of luck and you're a pony without prospects. It's *over*."

"What do you mean, Buck?" Bronco asked.

"I mean you were right," Buck growled. "We *never* should have come here. We'd be better off back at Happy Ranch among the dust and demolition trucks than ... than ..."

"Than rottin' in jail?" Bronco suggested.

"No, than being *forgotten*," replied Buck at last. "Turns out the rest of the world was changing, all that time we were at Happy Ranch. Now here we are in the town of the future and no one remembers us. No one even knows who we—"

"Buck 'n' Bronco?" said a voice.

The pair turned to see an alarmingly tall woman standing in the doorway. She had a sharp bob of blonde hair, silver-framed glasses and a massive bow tied on top of her head. She was dressed in a sky-blue suit that was the cleanest thing the mascots had ever seen.

"It's you ... it's *really* you," the woman said, her eyes wide and glinting.

"You ... you know who we are?" asked Bronco.

"Of course she doesn't," huffed Buck. "We're yesterday's mascots, remember?"

"Oh, but I *do*, deer," the woman chuckled. "How could I not know of the world's greatest theme-park mascots? Buck 'n' Bronco of Happy Ranch!"

"Wait, you really do *recognise* us?" Buck asked.

"Recognise you?" the woman said. "I feel like I've waited my whole life to see you again.

44

I spent the most delightful six hours of my childhood at Happy Ranch, riding the Rockin' Roller Coaster and the Happy Helter-Skelter. *Do the Buck 'n' Bronco dance! Fun, fun, fun at the Happy Ranch!* It was my happiest day! Who could have known that my time at Happy Ranch all those years ago would inspire my dream for tomorrow – the theme park of the future, today."

"Braid my main and feed me a sugar lump!" Bronco cried. "You're Alison Wunderland! Buck, it's the lady who knocked down Happy Ranch. Remember? You said you were goin' to give her a piece of your mind ..."

"Did I? I ... I don't rightly recall," Buck muttered, suddenly star-struck.

"I wouldn't blame you for being upset," Alison Wunderland said. She opened the door to their jail cell with the flick of a switch. "But with every ending comes a new beginning, does it not? So, while you are free to go, I very much hope you'll stay."

"Stay?" said Buck. "What do you mean?"

"Walk with me," Alison Wunderland replied, striding away. Buck 'n' Bronco raced out of the jail cell after her as she continued. "Tonight, I am holding a party at Wunderland Manor, where I will reveal the plans for my *new* theme park, Islands of Tomorrow. I've invited the whole town. Mine's the big, expensive-looking house on the hill, you can't miss it. There'll be snacks. Please, you *must* come."

"Us?" Bronco said, following Alison Wunderland out of the police station. The mascots watched a long silver car draw up to the roadside and the back door slide open.

"Of course – what's a theme park without mascots?" Alison Wunderland said, climbing into the car. "I have taken the liberty of filling up the Bronco Bus with laughing gas. You can hit the road tonight, if you want ... but I would be honoured if you would come to my party – as my very special guests."

Buck 'n' Bronco watched as the car pulled away and rounded a corner. There was a long moment of silence. Then:

"Cover me in mustard and call me a hot dog!" Buck cried. "Did you hear what she said? Very special guests! I should have known – Alison Wunderland wants us to be mascots for her new theme park!"

"Are you sure?" asked Bronco. "Shucks, Buck, I dunno ... That place is a whole lot shinier and more future-lookin' than the two of us."

"Don't overthink it, old pal," said Buck. "This is what we've been waiting for – Alison Wunderland is going to put us back on the mascot map. It's time to put the past behind us – we're heading to the Islands of Tomorrow!"

Chapter 7

Mascots of Tomorrow

*"If this is tomorrow, who wants to
live for today?"*

Buck spent the rest of the day getting ready for
the party at Wunderland Manor. He "pressed"
his waistcoat by driving the Bronco Bus over
it, flossed his teeth with a hair from Bronco's
mane and made sure his nose was well picked.

"A new life of fame awaits us, Bronco, old
buddy," Buck said as the Bronco Bus giggled
its way up the hill to the front gates of

Wunderland Manor. The sun had set and only the chirp of crickets and whirring of drones overhead could be heard.

Bronco did not reply. He was silent as he drove them past the gates and up the winding drive. They were greeted by a robot who parked the Bronco Bus and then another who welcomed them inside.

"Well, hang me on a peg and sell me in the gift shop!" laughed Buck, stepping through the huge double doors. "If this is tomorrow, who wants to live for today?"

Indeed, Wunderland Manor was a sight to behold. The silvery palace was *vast* and, despite the fact that the entire population of Wunderville seemed to be there, it had space to spare.

More robots ushered Buck 'n' Bronco outside into the back garden – an endless expanse of neat lawn. Townsfolk were already gathering round an enormous model of the Islands of Tomorrow theme park. It was as big as a swimming pool and filled with robotic rides, music, a laser show and even tiny robot people grinning as they lined up for rides.

Bronco saw the girl from the town square (still clutching her beloved blue balloon) and her family staring at the model, awestruck.

"It looks like the *future*," said Bronco, as impressed as he was nervous.

"It looks like *our* future, pal," added Buck with a grin. "It looks like—"

"The Islands of Tomorrow!" someone cried. Buck 'n' Bronco glanced back to see Alison Wunderland striding out of the house. "Welcome, one and all, to my most ambitious project ever!" she went on, her voice booming thanks to the microphone drones hovering around her. "In six months' time, the Islands of Tomorrow will welcome visitors from all over the world to the most spectacular theme park ever imagined. But one thing's still missing that all great theme parks need ... well, two things, actually. For what is a theme park without its mascots?"

"This is it, Bronco – we're back in the spotlight ... back in business!" Buck whispered, nudging his friend in the knee.

"I've got a bad feeling about this, Buck," murmured Bronco. A moment later, more robots ushered Buck 'n' Bronco out of the crowd towards Alison Wunderland.

"May I present my very special guests ... a blast from the past ... the mascots of yesterday, it's Buck 'n' Bronco!" Wunderland declared.

"It's happening!" squealed Buck. "Our luck is finally ... Wait, did she say *yesterday*?"

"For years, these marvellous mascots represented the Happy Ranch theme park ..."

Alison Wunderland continued. "But that was a long time ago. Today, we bid farewell to the past and usher in the future ..."

"The future? What's she talking about?" whispered Buck as Bronco put his head in his hands.

"Friends, I give you Buck 'n' Bronco's successors!" Alison Wunderland cried. "The mascots of tomorrow, Zero and One!"

"Who ...?" whimpered Buck.

The girl with the balloon gasped.

Strange glimmering figures appeared out of thin air each side of Alison Wunderland. They were more or less human sized but formed of boxy shapes made entirely of light.

"I'm your hero, Zero!" Zero said with a shimmering wink.

"And I'm the one and only One!" added One. Laughter rang out across the crowd.

"Zero and One are *virtual* mascots," explained Alison Wunderland as she swept her arms through the holographic forms of Zero and One. "They can upload themselves to any of the many rides and experiences at the Islands of Tomorrow. Zero and One will monitor your satisfaction levels at every moment and tailor your experience to ensure that you're having as much fun as possible."

"But I thought ... she said ... I was so sure ..." Buck began, tears suddenly stinging his eyes.

Bronco put his hand on his friend's shoulder.

"I'm sorry, Buck – I think our mascot days may be done," Bronco said with a sniff. "But that doesn't mean we can't still try to Bring the Happy."

"Doesn't it …?" Buck replied, with a sigh as long and sad as had ever been sighed. "I don't think I have it in me any more, Bronco. I don't care if I never Bring the Happy ever again."

Buck turned his back – on Alison Wunderland, on the Islands of Tomorrow, on the townsfolk, even on his best friend – and walked away.

"W-where are you goin', Buck?" asked Bronco. "Buck? Come back! Buck!"

But Buck wandered down the garden and vanished into the night.

Chapter 8
The Balloon

*"With a little help from my best
friend, I can do anythin'."*

"Come back, Buck!" Bronco called out after his
friend. "Buck! Come—"

"B'loon!" someone yelped.

Bronco glanced back towards the crowd.
The cry had come from the girl with the blue
balloon ... except she didn't have it. A gust of

wind had blown the balloon from her hand. It was floating up into the air.

"B'loon!" howled the girl. "Come back, b'loon!"

Another gust blew the balloon towards Zero and One, but the mascots' holographic hands went right through it.

"You are Zero help," One tutted.

"You're One to talk," Zero huffed.

"B'loon! Come back!" the girl cried again, tears welling in her eyes. As the balloon floated higher, the drones above moved away to avoid bursting it with their rotor blades.

"Aw, *no*," said Bronco, and galloped into the darkness after his friend. "Buck! Where are you at? We gotta help! We gotta— Uff!"

Bronco ran straight into Buck, sending the pair of them tumbling to the ground in a mess of tangled arms and legs.

"There – oww – you are!" Bronco gasped, his head trapped between Buck's antlers. "Buck, just the worst, most awful thing has happened!"

"How could this day *possibly* get any worse?" Buck moaned as he pulled Bronco's left foot out of his ear.

"That girl from the square lost her balloon!" Bronco yelled. "We gotta get it back!"

"Why?" huffed Buck. "Saving some stupid balloon is not going to get us our jobs back, Bronco. It's not going to make us mascots again."

"That is true," Bronco agreed. He glanced back up the hill at the girl. She was trying to wipe the tears out of her eyes before they rolled down her cheeks. "But it might – just *might* – Bring the Happy to that girl over there."

"One kid?" Buck groaned. "What's the point of Bringing the Happy to—"

"*Cos that's what we do!*" cried Bronco. "Cos even if that's all we ever do – even if we only Bring the Happy to one more person – ain't that worth it? Ain't that what Buck 'n' Bronco do?"

Buck gazed up into the night sky and saw the girl's blue balloon floating ever higher.

"I ... I guess it is," he said. "So, what do you want me to do?"

Bronco sniffed.

"Pull my finger," he said.

Bronco held his index finger out. Buck took hold of the finger and then looked up. By now the balloon was so far above them, he could barely see it.

"Are you sure?" asked Buck.

"You know I can't break wind unless you pull my finger, Buck," Bronco said.

"No, I mean, are you sure you can make it?" said Buck. "That balloon is real high in the sky."

"With a little help from my best friend, I can do anythin'," Bronco replied.

Buck nodded ... smiled ... and pulled.

PAAAAARRRRRP!

The crowd gasped in amazement as they saw Bronco shoot high into the air. The sound of his forceful fart rang out across the garden, Wunderville and beyond.

Buck crossed his fingers as his friend vanished into the night sky. For a long moment, there was silence. Buck suddenly wondered if his friend was ever going to come down. Then:

"Look out beloowww!" cried a voice from above.

With a

FWEEEEEEEEEEEEEEE –

DOIMP!

Bronco hit the ground.

"Buck! I got it!" said Bronco, dazed as he held out the girl's blue balloon. "Buck ...?"

"Good ... catch ..." Buck wheezed in reply.

Bronco looked down to see Buck squashed flat beneath him, his feet sticking out of the bottom and antlers poking out of the top.

"Shucks, Buck, I sure do appreciate the soft landing," said Bronco. "An' I think *you* should do the honours with the balloon."

"Me? But—" Buck began, but Bronco tied the blue balloon's thread around Buck's antler.

"Go ahead," said Bronco. "Bring the Happy."

The crowd watched in stunned silence as the flattened Buck waddled up the garden over to the girl. He managed to stick his fingers up his nostrils and – with a sudden POP! – returned to his normal shape. The girl giggled and wiped away the last of her tears.

"Lose something?" Buck said with a smile. Then he took the balloon off his antler and handed it to the girl.

"B'loon!" the girl cried, tears of joy replacing her tears of sadness. "You got b'loon!"

"And I'm honoured to return it to you," replied Buck. "You take care of that, now. It looks like a very *special* balloon."

"It's my first b'loon ever," the girl said, wiping her tears from her eyes as she grinned from ear to ear. "This is my happiest day!"

Buck smiled and blinked away a happy tear of his own.

"Well, isn't that something?" he said. "It's mine, too."

Chapter 9
Bringing the Happy

"Truth is, I think I forgot what being Buck 'n' Bronco really means."

The gathered townsfolk clapped and cheered as Buck returned the girl's balloon. Shouts of "Buck 'n' Bronco! Buck 'n' Bronco!" filled the air.

"Braid my mane and feed me a sugar lump," Bronco said as he trotted up behind Buck. "Would you look at that?"

"They know ... they know who we are!" said Buck. "We're *famous* again."

"After all those years, you've still got that mascot magic," said Alison Wunderland, striding over to Buck 'n' Bronco. "Perhaps I was too hasty, relegating you to the past. Perhaps there is a place in the Islands of Tomorrow for a little slice of yesterday. Buck 'n' Bronco, how would you like your very own theme park within a theme park? A sort of Happy Ranch of the Future?"

"You ... you'd do that?" Buck blurted. "You'd build us a new Happy Ranch?"

"Why not? It could be just like the old days," replied Alison Wunderland. "How about it?"

Buck grinned so wide he showed every tooth in his mouth. But then he looked over to Bronco and saw his friend's tail swishing worriedly.

"What do you say, old buddy?" Buck asked. Bronco ruffled his mane.

"I say … if it makes you happy, it makes me happy," Bronco replied with a weak smile.

"Well, dip me in batter and call me a corn dog! Buck 'n' Bronco are back in business!" cried Buck. "We're finally … back … in …"

Buck trailed off as he glanced over at the girl beaming brightly with her balloon. Then he looked back at Bronco, who was trying his best to keep smiling. Buck sighed and rubbed the back of his head.

"Well?" said Alison Wunderland. "Do we have a deal?"

Buck pointed at his rump.

"You see that, Ms Wunderland?" he said.

"… Your butt?" said Alison Wunderland.

"No, *that*," Buck said. He poked the letters "B&B" on his backside. "Truth is, I think I forgot what being Buck 'n' Bronco really means," Buck continued. "We didn't set out to be famous. Heck, we didn't even set out to be mascots. We just wanted to Bring the Happy ... and that's why I'm going to have to turn down your kind offer."

"*What?*" gasped Alison Wunderland and Bronco together.

"From now on, Buck 'n' Bronco are going to Bring the Happy to anyone who needs it," Buck went on. "Not in a theme park, but out there in the world beyond Happy Ranch ... in the *real* world."

"Shucks, Buck, you really mean it?" asked Bronco, happy tears welling in his eyes (and nostrils). "What about the spotlight? What about being mascots again?"

"That was then," said Buck. "This is now."

"No one has ever said 'no' to me before," Alison Wunderland admitted. "It makes me feel rather unwell. However, I admire your decision and I wish you the very best of luck. You have ten minutes to get out of town before I set my Wundercops on you."

Buck 'n' Bronco wasted no time in hopping back on the Bronco Bus. They rode out of the gates of Wunderland Manor and down the hill, and kept driving until Wunderville was far behind them.

They drove all through the night, until the sun began to peek over the horizon. And for the longest time, they didn't say a word. Then, at last:

"Thank you, Buck," said Bronco. "I know you wanted to be a mascot again more than anything."

"No, thank *you*, Bronco," Buck replied. "You made me remember who we are and what we do. We're Buck 'n' Bronco, and we Bring the Happy."

Bronco smiled as the rising sun lit up the world.

"So what now, Buck?" he asked. "Where to?"

"Wherever the road leads, old friend," replied Buck.

"You got it," Bronco chuckled. He stepped on the laughing-gas pedal, and the Bronco Bus chuckled too. "Oh, and Buck? Would you mind doin' me a favour?"

"Bronco, you know you just have to ask," replied Buck. "What can I do for you?"

Bronco grinned.

"Pull my finger."

Guy Bass

NOAH SCAPE CAN'T STOP REPEATING HIMSELF

978-1-78112-772-8

Guy Bass

ANNA GAIN

...NDS

978-1-78112-916-6

Winner of the Blue Peter Book Award

Guy Bass

AIDAN ABET TEACHER'S PET

Guy Bass

LAURA NORDER

SHERIFF OF BUTTS CANYON

978-1-78412-845-9

Our books are tested
for children and young people by
children and young people.

Thanks to everyone who consulted on
a manuscript for their time and effort in
helping us to make our books better
for our readers.